Boat on the river
Row me away . . .

For Dante,
my poemboy

Copyright © 2001 by Camilla Ashforth
First U.S. edition 2002
Library of Congress Cataloging-in-Publication Data
Ashforth, Camilla.
Willow on the river / Camilla Ashforth. — 1st U.S. ed.
p.   cm.
Summary: After doing his chores around the farm, Willow sets off for a
day of fun rowing, picnicking, and playing on the river.
ISBN 0-7636-1088-7
[1. Teddy bears — Fiction. 2. Country life — Fiction.] I. Title.
PZ7.A823 Wi 2001
[E] — dc21   99-087637

2 4 6 8 10 9 7 5 3 1

Printed in Italy

This book was typeset in Columbus.
The illustrations were done in watercolor and pencil.

Candlewick Press
2067 Massachusetts Avenue
Cambridge, Massachusetts 02140

WILLOW

on the River

Camilla Ashforth

CANDLEWICK PRESS
CAMBRIDGE, MASSACHUSETTS

The gentlest bear you ever will meet
is Willow.

He lives at the foot of the Appleby Downs
where Paradise Fields meet the river.

PARADISE FARM

One morning Willow looked out from his barn.
"I must spend today on the river."

First, he had to work on the farm.
Little Pig Pink tried to help him.

They fed the cows, the horse, and the goat.

They gathered the geese in the yard.

They moved the sheep to the meadow fields.

They hunted for eggs in the henhouse.

Then Willow went in and
made up a picnic.

He carried it down
to the river.

Little Pig Pink watched from the shore
as Willow pushed out his boat.

"Look after the farm while I'm away," called Willow.
Little Pig Pink said, "Oink."

As Willow rowed he sang a song:

Boat on the river,
Row me away.
There'll be a bank
Where I can play;
A pool where I'll paddle,
A tree I can climb,
A meadow to run through
Till picnic time.

At Anyan Bank, Willow met Finley,
skipping stones from the sandy shore.

"Lovely day," Finley called.
"Come for a picnic?" cried Willow.

ANYAN BANK

Willow and Finley rowed together and
talked of farms and fishing.

ULLSHAW BRIDGE

The river widens at Ullshaw Bridge
and runs into pools by the rocks.
Together the bears pulled the boat in
and took out the picnic for later.

Then in the shallows Finley paddled
while Willow hunted for treasure.

They made a dam across the river
and floated fleets of leaves.

They leapt and sprang from rock to rock

and swung above the water.

After play they ate their picnic, sitting in the meadow.

Cucumber sandwiches, cupcakes, and chips.

Apples and elderflower punch.

Then Willow and Finley
lay back in the grass, watching clouds
and blowing dandelion wishes.

The sun was setting when they turned
the boat and Willow took Finley home.

Boat on the water,
Row us away
Here at the end
Of a lovely day.
We played in the meadow
And down by the shore;
One day soon
We'll play some more.

Little Pig Pink was waiting for Willow
when he got back to the farm.

"Good night, chickens," Willow said.

"Good night, sheep and cows."

"Good night, horse and good night, geese."

"Sleep well, Little Pig Pink."

Willow looked out at the moonlit view
of the fields and the river beyond. Then
he lay back in bed and closed his eyes.

Moonshine on Paradise,
Stars on the stream,
A breeze through the treetops
To whisper a dream.

Willow's River Song

Boat on the ri - ver, Row me a - way.

There'll be a bank Where I can play; A

pool where I'll pad-dle, A tree I can climb, A

mea - dow to run through Till pic - nic time.